ONE DIRECTION

Test Your Super-Fan Status

New Edition

Written by Nicola Baxter
and Jen Wainwright

Edited by Jen Wainwright
Design by Barbara Ward
Cover design by Zoe Bradley

Picture Acknowledgements:
Front cover: Jon Furniss/Invision for Children in Need/
AP Images
Picture section:
Page 1, David Fisher/Rex Features
Page 2, Matt Baron/BEI/Rex Features
Page 3, Getty Images
Page 4, Matt Baron/BEI/Rex Features
Page 5, Matt Baron/BEI/Rex Features
Pages 6–7, John Marshall/Invision/
Press Association Images
Page 8, Sara Jaye/Rex Features

First edition for North America published in 2013
by Barron's Educational Series, Inc.

First published in Great Britain in 2013 by Buster Books,
an imprint of Michael O'Mara Books Limited,
9 Lion Yard, Tremadoc Road, London SW4 7NQ

www.busterbooks.co.uk

Text copyright © Buster Books 2013

Artwork adapted from *www.shutterstock.com*

All inquiries should be addressed to:
Barron's Educational Series, Inc.
250 Wireless Boulevard
Hauppauge, NY 11788
www.barronseduc.com

**PLEASE NOTE: This book is not affiliated with or endorsed by One Direction
or any of their publishers or licensees.**

ISBN: 978-1-4380-0373-3

Library of Congress Control No.: 2013940134

Date of Manufacture: June 2013
Manufactured by: B12V12G

Printed in the United States of America

9 8 7 6 5 4 3 2 1

ONE DIRECTION

Test Your Super-Fan Status

New Edition

CONTENTS

About This Book 5

Super-Fan-Tastic 6

Fact File: Harry Styles 9

Direction Detection! 10

Who Said It? 12

Number Knowledge 15

Tattoo Trivia 16

Spot The Fakes 18

Hot Horoscopes 20

Crack That Crossword 24

Mystery Tweeter 26

Get Jet-Set 27

How Romantic 28

Video Stars 30

Helping Hands 32

Fact File: Niall Horan 35

Every Direction 36

Around The World 38

Mystery Tweeter 41

Would You Rather? 42

Who's Your 1D 44
Style Icon?

Bad Boys 46

Fact File: Liam Payne 48

Mystery Tweeter 49

Setlist Scramble 50

Seriously Spooky 52

Secret Gig 56

Big Dreams 58

The Blush Factor 62

Fact File: Louis 65
Tomlinson

Quiz Time 66

Mystery Tweeter 69

Who's Your 1D BFF? 70

Fact File: Zayn Malik 72

The Fame Game 73

Bowling Boys 78

Fan Frenzy 82

Name That Tune 84

Center Stage 86

Mystery Tweeter 88

All The Answers 89

ABOUT THIS BOOK

It's official, you've got a bad case of One Direction infection. You know their hit songs by heart, love to dance to their videos with your BFFs, and you could happily spend hours gazing at their gorgeous faces.

Whether you've been a fan since the beginning when they burst onto the scene on *The X Factor,* or if they've caught your eye after with their catchy melodies and stunning smiles, you've fallen head over heels for the boys.

So, just how much do you know about your five fave guys? This book is packed with tricky trivia, crosswords, puzzles, and quizzes to put you to the test.

Are you ready for the challenge? If so, grab a pen and follow the instructions at the top of each page—you can check your answers on **pages 89 to 95**. Get the latest info on the coolest boy band ever and discover what type of One Direction fan you really are.

SUPER-FAN-TASTIC

GET READY TO FIND OUT JUST HOW MUCH OF A DIRECTIONER YOU REALLY ARE, WITH THIS QUIZ FULL OF TRICKY 1D TRIVIA. CHECK YOUR ANSWERS ON **PAGE 89**.

1. Who is the youngest member of the band?
- a. Liam
- b. Louis
- c. Harry

2. In which year was the band formed?
- a. 2009
- b. 2011
- c. 2010

3. Which member of One Direction created his stage name by changing the spelling of his original name?
- a. Zayn
- b. Niall
- c. Louis

4. Which band was Harry in before he joined One Direction?
   a. White Lightning
   b. White Eskimo
   c. White Seagull

5. Only one band member has a brother. Which one?
   a. Louis
   b. Zayn
   c. Niall

6. When asked to choose a theme song for the band, what did Harry suggest?
   a. "Wouldn't It Be Nice"
   b. "Thriller"
   c. "The Boys Are Back In Town"

7. One Direction won Favorite Song at the 2013 Nickelodeon Kids' Choice Awards with which hit song?
   a. "Little Things"
   b. "What Makes You Beautiful"
   c. "Live While We're Young"

8. What is the name of the band's first 3D movie?
   a. One Dream, 1D
   b. Come With Us
   c. This Is Us

9. Which One Direction video was filmed in black and white?
- **a.** "Little Things"
- **b.** "One Way Or Another"
- **c.** "Gotta Be You"

10. Which British singer-songwriter co-wrote One Direction's "Moments?"
- **a.** Paul McCartney
- **b.** Ed Sheeran
- **c.** Gary Barlow

11. What do the boys say is the hardest part about being in the most successful boy band in the world?
- **a.** Spending so much time with each other
- **b.** Missing their friends and family
- **c.** Getting recognized everywhere they go

12. Two of the boys share the same middle name. What is it?
- **a.** Edward
- **b.** David
- **c.** James

ONE DIRECTION!

FACT FILE: HARRY STYLES

ONLY FOUR OF THESE FIVE STATEMENTS ABOUT HARRY ARE TRUE. PUT A CHECK IN THE BOX BESIDE EACH STATEMENT THAT YOU THINK IS TRUE. PUT AN "X" NEXT TO EACH STATEMENT THAT YOU THINK IS FALSE. THE ANSWERS ARE ON **PAGE 89**.

1. Harry is from Cheshire.

2. Harry's favorite vegetable is sweetcorn.

3. Harry's astrological sign is Aquarius.

4. Harry's hair isn't naturally curly. He curls it with a curling iron.

5. Harry came up with the name One Direction.

DIRECTION DETECTION!

UP, DOWN, FORWARD, BACKWARD, EVEN DIAGONALLY—YOU NEED TO SEARCH EVERY WHICH WAY IN THIS PUZZLE. CAN YOU FIND THE WORDS THAT BELONG TO THE WONDERFUL WORLD OF ONE DIRECTION? TURN TO **PAGE 89** IF YOU GET STUCK.

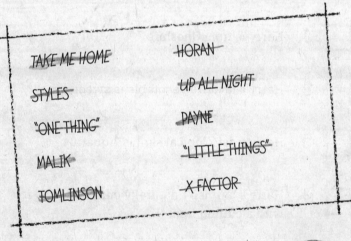

TAKE ME HOME

STYLES

"ONE THING"

MALIK

TOMLINSON

HORAN

UP ALL NIGHT

PAYNE

"LITTLE THINGS"

X FACTOR

P	A	N	E	R	H	J	K	L	I	M	A	S	E	F
L	I	T	T	L	E	T	H	I	N	G	S	O	N	E
N	Y	O	M	F	T	A	L	C	T	A	K	I	H	T
L	N	M	G	N	I	L	M	B	A	E	E	F	O	Z
G	A	L	C	A	K	P	H	S	K	A	M	A	S	A
N	D	I	H	G	I	N	U	P	E	D	G	G	Y	Y
A	O	N	E	T	H	I	N	G	M	L	A	J	T	R
W	H	S	L	N	X	F	A	T	E	L	Y	P	L	O
R	A	O	I	R	D	H	O	N	H	O	F	T	T	T
F	R	N	T	E	A	M	Y	L	O	L	D	J	S	C
S	R	J	T	E	A	A	D	R	M	L	P	F	L	A
T	O	X	P	O	P	Y	B	W	E	R	M	E	I	F
H	O	R	A	N	Z	Q	M	O	R	A	N	F	K	X
E	R	T	H	G	I	N	L	L	A	P	U	I	U	Q
S	A	E	P	O	T	N	O	U	K	I	L	A	M	Z

WHO SAID IT?

OK, SUPER-FAN, IT'S TIME TO TEST YOUR SKILLS AND SEE IF YOU CAN FIGURE OUT WHICH OF THE GUYS IS SPEAKING. READ THE QUOTES FROM THE 1D BOYS AND FILL IN WHO SAID EACH ONE. THE ANSWERS ARE ON **PAGE 90**.

1. "Obviously our everyday lives have changed, but I honestly can't see any of us ever getting big-headed or thinking we're special—there's too much banter between us for that to happen!"

Who said it? ...... *Niall*

2. "The one movie that made me cry—it's got to be *Marley & Me*—it's just a sad movie about a really nice dog."

Who said it? ...... *Liam*

3. "I've always wanted to be one of those people who didn't really care that much about what people thought about them, but I just don't think I am."

Who said it? ...... *Harry Styles*

4. "It makes a huge difference to be able to sing something that you've helped create."

Who said it? ...... *Niall* ....

5. "We couldn't compare what we do with what the British athletes did at the Olympics."

Who said it? ...... *Louis* ....

6. "When I was about eight, I had a dream that a giant Power Ranger was chasing me around."

Who said it? ...... *Zayn* ....

7. "I'd say I was quite shy, although it doesn't look it when there's cameras and stuff. But if I ask a star for a photo with them, I'm not very good at all. I just haven't got the confidence."

Who said it? ...... *Liam* ....

8. "Somebody once made me a teddy bear of my girlfriend, which was quite cute, I thought."

Who said it? ...... *Liam* ....

9. "Once I shaved off Louis's eyebrows and then Louis shaved off Liam's and then Harry shaved his initials into the hairs on my leg while I was asleep."

Who said it? _Zayn_

10. "In some ways we are like students in the way we live, except that we work harder."

Who said it? _Liam._

11. "I love a girl in a dress and Converse."

Who said it? _Harry_

12. "Harry won't change his hair until he goes bald."

Who said it? _Louis._

13. "We would love to collaborate with Katy Perry. That's a dream."

Who said it? _Louis_

14. "When you're on *The X Factor*, just enjoy yourself, and when you do come off, keep grounded."

Who said it? _Niall._

NUMBER KNOWLEDGE

YOU MIGHT BE THE BOYS' NUMBER ONE FAN, BUT ARE YOU NUMBER ONE AT PLAYING THE 1D NUMBERS GAME? TEST YOUR NUMBER KNOWLEDGE BY READING THE STATEMENTS BELOW AND MATCHING THEM WITH THE CORRECT NUMBERS LISTED AT THE BOTTOM OF THE PAGE. CHECK YOUR ANSWERS ON **PAGE 90**.

1. Tracks on the original *Take Me Home* album: 13

2. Highest singles chart position reached: 1

3. Minutes in which their tour of Australia and New Zealand sold out: 3

4. Cities performed in on 1D's first US tour: 21

5. Number of countries 1D's debut album *Up All Night* was number one in: 15

6. 1D boys with the astrological sign Virgo: 2

1   **3**   **2**

  15   **13**   **21**

TATTOO TRIVIA

THERE'S NO DOUBT THAT THOSE ONE DIRECTION BOYS ARE CREATIVE, BUT IT'S NOT JUST THROUGH THEIR MUSIC THAT THEY LIKE TO EXPRESS THEMSELVES. EVER SINCE THEY GOT TOGETHER, THEY'VE BEEN ASSEMBLING AN IMPRESSIVE COLLECTION OF TATTOOS. CAN YOU IDENTIFY EACH BOY BELOW BY HIS INKED ART? TURN TO **PAGE 90** TO SEE IF YOU'RE RIGHT.

1. This 1D member is making sure we hear him loud and clear with a life-sized microphone on his arm.

Whose tatt is that? ...... Zayn ......

2. Well, you already know he's a star, but he has one tattooed on his arm anyway.

Whose tatt is that? ...... Harry Styles ......

3. Always on the move, this guy has a stick figure on a skateboard on his forearm.

Whose tatt is that? ...... Louis Tomlinson ......

4. The phrase "Be true to who you are" is written in Arabic on this philosophical boy's body.

Whose tatt is that? _Zayn Malik_

5. Since shooting to superstardom, this boy has blossomed like a beautiful butterfly—which is handy, as he now has one tattooed on his stomach.

Whose tatt is that? _Harry Styles_

6. This down-to-earth sweetheart makes a bold statement with a series of big, black arrows called chevrons on his forearm.

Whose tatt is that? _Liam Payne_

7. Maybe it's to remind him of something embarrassing he did in the past, or maybe it's an advance apology for something in the future. Either way, this tattoo spells "OOPS!"

Whose tatt is that? _Louis Tomlinson_

8. This 1D guy likes to keep things mysterious, with a tatt that reads "Only time will tell ..."

Whose tatt is that? _Liam._

SPOT THE FAKES

READ THESE STATEMENTS ABOUT ONE DIRECTION, THEN DECIDE IF THEY ARE TRUE OR FALSE. CHECK THE BOXES TO MARK YOUR ANSWERS, THEN TURN TO **PAGE 90** TO FIND OUT HOW YOU DID.

1. Harry supports Manchester United Football Club.

☑ True   ☐ False

2. Niall hurt his knee when he was attacked by a squirrel.

☐ True   ☑ False

3. The first track on *Take Me Home* is "Kiss You."

☐ True   ☑ False

4. Louis is claustrophobic—he panics when he's in a confined space.

☐ True   ☑ False

5. Zayn has three sisters.

☑ True   ☐ False

6. Harry was eighteen when he had his first kiss.

☐ True   ☑ False

7. Three of the boys have brown eyes.

☐ True ☑ False

8. The 1D boys like to swallow spoonfuls of honey before performing to help their voices stay strong.

☐ True ☑ False

9. One Direction is the first U.K. band in history to enter the U.S. chart at number one with their debut album.

☑ True ☐ False

10. The boys' moms love their tattoos.

☐ True ☑ False

11. Niall gets more marriage proposals than any of the other boys.

☑ True ☐ False

12. The band's first 3D film is called *This Is It*.

☐ True ☑ False

13. Louis would love to go into space.

☑ True ☐ False

14. One of Liam's grandfathers was Portuguese.

☐ True ☑ False

15. Niall has not yet passed his driving test.

☐ True ☑ False

HOT HOROSCOPES

FIND YOUR HOROSCOPE AND DISCOVER WHAT IT SAYS ABOUT YOU. THEN, FIND OUT WHICH OF THE GORGEOUS ONE DIRECTION BOYS YOU'RE MOST LIKE. WHY NOT COMPARE YOUR RESULTS WITH YOUR FRIENDS, TOO?

ARIES (MARCH 21 – APRIL 19)

You like: The great outdoors, parties, exotic food

You don't like: Having to be patient, team sports, libraries

You're most like Louis: Just like Mr. Tomlinson, you're not afraid to take the lead when things need to get done, and you're happiest when surrounded by your friends.

TAURUS (APRIL 20 – MAY 20)

You like: Helping others, shopping sprees, sleepovers

You don't like: Lateness, drama, bossiness

You're most like Liam: Liam's often known as the sensible one of the band, and, like you, he takes care of the people close to him. You've both got a good sense of humor though, and you're not afraid to be a bit silly when the mood strikes you.

GEMINI (MAY 21 – JUNE 21)

You like: Adventures, meeting new people

You don't like: Feeling left out, being on your own

You're most like Harry: Harry's your closest match because he's happy to throw himself into any new situation and get the best out of it with a smile on his face, just like you.

CANCER (JUNE 22 – JULY 22)

You like: Being close to family, reading, nature

You don't like: Feeling out of control, forgetfulness

You're most like Zayn: You and Zayn have a lot in common. Like you, his family are really important to him, and he loves to spend time at home chilling out with them. You can both be a bit shy in new situations, but once you feel comfortable you'll soon relax and have fun.

LEO (JULY 23– AUGUST 22)

You like: Luxury, being independent, loud music

You don't like: Being fussed over, moody people

You're most like Niall: Your sunny personality and infectious grin means you're most like 1D's Irish charmer. Like Niall, you can be the life and soul of any party if you want to be, but you're equally happy on your sofa, relaxing with some DVDs. As long as you don't feel under pressure, you'll be enjoying yourself.

VIRGO (AUGUST 23 – SEPTEMBER 22)

You like: Long walks, art, solving problems

You don't like: People getting upset, spontaneity

You're most like Zayn: You and Zayn are both pretty deep thinkers—you like life to be calm, and you hate it when people panic about things. You can be counted upon to keep your head cool in a crisis.

LIBRA (SEPTEMBER 23 – OCTOBER 22)

You like: Beach holidays, making people laugh

You don't like: Early mornings, scruffy people

You're most like Louis: You and Louis are both seriously stylish people. You like to look your best at all times, and your easygoing nature means you're always good fun to be around. You hate making too many plans, and would prefer to just go with the flow.

SCORPIO (OCTOBER 23 – NOVEMBER 21)

You like: Exciting new ideas, bright colors, dancing

You don't like: Being bored, routines, laziness

You're most like Niall: You and Niall can both be perfectionists. You're not afraid to say what you want and to go out and get it, and you'll charm anyone you meet, so it's likely that you'll get your own way.

SAGITTARIUS (NOVEMBER 22 – DECEMBER 21)

You like: Tidiness, animals, meaningful conversations

You don't like: Irrational people, not saying what you mean

You're most like Liam: Most of the time, you have a sunny personality, but you can occasionally be short-tempered when you feel stressed, just like Liam. You like to have your own space, and it's very important to you that your friends understand you and that you feel connected to them.

CAPRICORN (DECEMBER 22 – JANUARY 19)
You like: Learning new skills, sightseeing
You don't like: Surprises, not feeling prepared for a task
You're most like Liam: Both you and Liam love to be in control of things. You're great fun to be around, but you like to have life planned in advance and feel uncomfortable if things are sprung on you.

AQUARIUS (JANUARY 20 – FEBRUARY 18)
You like: Festivals, travel, feeling challenged
You don't like: Being judged, following the crowd
You're most like Harry: Just like 1D's curly-haired cutie, you're a little bit quirky and you dare to be different. Your friends admire your carefree attitude and sense of style.

PISCES (FEBRUARY 19 – MARCH 20)
You like: Daydreaming, writing stories, quiet time
You don't like: Tactless people, pranks
You're most like Zayn: Zayn's sensitive side is the part of him that you can relate to most. You're thoughtful and creative, but you can get upset easily.

CRACK THAT CROSSWORD

READ THE CLUES BELOW AND SEE HOW QUICKLY YOU CAN WRITE YOUR ANSWERS IN THE CROSSWORD GRID ON THE OPPOSITE PAGE CHECK OUT THE ANSWERS ON **PAGE 91** WHEN YOU'RE DONE.

ACROSS

1. Last name of the band's youngest member (6)

4. One Direction video directed by Declan Whitebloom (3, 5)

5. Name of 1D's second album (4, 2, 4)

6. British Prime Minister appearing in the video for "One Way Or Another" (5, 7)

7. Band that originally released "One Way Or Another" (7)

DOWN

1. Music and television production company that One Direction are signed to (4)

2. Song co-written by Ed Sheeran (6, 6)

3. Band member inside the telephone booth on the cover of 5 Across (5, 5)

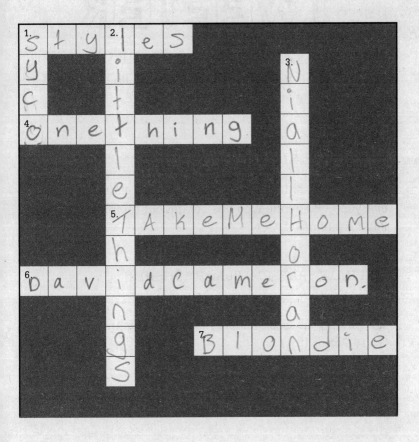

MYSTERY TWEETER

CAN YOU GUESS WHO WROTE THESE SWEET TWEETS? WRITE YOUR ANSWER AT THE BOTTOM OF THE PAGE, THEN CHECK **PAGE 91** TO SEE IF YOU WERE RIGHT.

🐦 Ahhhhh I'm 21 !!

......*Louis Tomlinson*......................................

🐦 The biggest thank you possible in 140 characters to everyone worldwide who has bought our album and single. You inspire us!

....

🐦 I HATE TRAFFIC !! BLAAHHHHHHHH

....

🐦 Having the most amazing lazy day watching Harry Potter !!!

....

🐦 Little unknown fact for you all I once did a film with Eddie Redmayne, I was an extra ha! :)

The mystery Tweeter is ......*Louis Tomlinson*.......

GET JET-SET

THOSE GORGEOUS ONE DIRECTION BOYS MAKE THEIR DIRECTIONERS SWOON WHEREVER THEY GO. READ ON TO FIND OUT HOW TO PROCLAIM YOUR LOVE FOR THE BOYS NO MATTER WHERE THEY ARE.

Here's how to say "I love One Direction" ...

... in French: J'adore One Direction

... in Spanish: Me encanta One Direction

... in German: Ich liebe One Direction

... in Italian: Amo gli One Direction

... in Swedish: Jag älskar One Direction

... in Dutch: Ik hou van One Direction

... in Portuguese: Eu amo One Direction

HOW ROMANTIC

THE 1D BOYS MIGHT WANT TO BE COOL AS CUCUMBERS AT ALL TIMES, BUT UNDERNEATH THEY'RE ALL REAL SOFTIES WITH HEARTS OF GOLD. READ THE GESTURES, STORIES, AND MISHAPS ABOUT 1D AND ROMANCE, THEN FILL IN WHO YOU THINK EACH ONE OF THEM IS ABOUT. YOU CAN FIND THE ANSWERS ON **PAGE 91**.

1. This boy's heart-meltingly cute plan for romance involved setting up lots of candles on a bridge near his crush's house. Unfortunately, the plan backfired when the girl he liked said it was too dark and she didn't want to come out of her house.

Answer: _Harry_

2. Which shy guy thought that people would be able to tell just by looking at him that he'd been kissed for the first time?

Answer: _Zayn_

3. Who bought a puppy with his girlfriend and named it Loki?

Answer: _Liam Payne_

4. Who once hired a rowing boat and rowed his crush out on a lake while singing romantic songs to her?

Answer: .... *Niall.* ....

5. It seems impossible to believe, but which guy once had a girl break things off with him because he wasn't good looking enough for her?

Answer: .... *Louis.* ....

6. Which thoughtful gent is reported to have scoured shops for a beautiful emerald bracelet that he knew his girlfriend at the time would adore?

Answer: .... *Harry.* ....

7. This 1D cutie has spoken about his love of girls who have brains, saying, "Someone can be the best looking person in the world, but if they're boring there's nothing worse. You have to have something to stimulate you mentally."

Answer: .... *Zayn* ....

8. He says he's not much of a cook, but which guy whipped up a romantic meal of chicken stuffed with mozzarella cheese and wrapped in ham for a girl he liked?

Answer: .... *Louis.* ....

VIDEO STARS

ONE OF THE BOYS' FAVORITE THINGS ABOUT BEING IN ONE DIRECTION IS THEIR VIDEO SHOOTS. THEY LOVE HAVING FUN TOGETHER ON CAMERA AND VISITING LOTS OF COOL LOCATIONS.

SO HOW MUCH DO YOU KNOW ABOUT THE VIDEOS AND THE SHOOTS THAT CREATED THEM? READ THE STATEMENTS BELOW, AND SEE IF YOU CAN FIGURE OUT WHICH VIDEO EACH ONE IS REFERRING TO. YOU CAN FIND THE ANSWERS ON **PAGE 91.**

1. This super-fun video includes a crazy downhill race between three of the boys on ball hoppers.

Which vid is it? _One Thing_

2. During the shoot of this video in California, Harry fell asleep on the beach, and Zayn buried him in the sand!

Which vid is it? _What Makes You Beautiful_

3. It's not every band that could persuade the Prime Minister of the U.K. to appear in their music video, but that's just what those 1D boys did.

Which vid is it? _One Way or Another_
(Teenage Kicks)

4. The boys all agree that this video shoot was great fun, but Louis ended up in a bit of trouble after he managed to break the jeep he was driving on the shoot. Oops!

Which vid is it? *Live While Wer're Young*

5. This video was shot at Lake Placid in upstate New York. It's a beautiful setting, but poor Liam was scared that there were crocodiles in the lake.

Which vid is it? *Gotta Be You.*

6. As far as you're concerned, One Direction rule the music scene, but in one video they all impersonate the King of Rock'n'Roll, Elvis Presley, in his famous shoot for "Jailhouse Rock."

Which vid is it? *Kiss You*

7. This arty video is all shot in black and white, and shows the boys relaxing in a recording studio and strumming on guitars.

Which vid is it? *Little Things*

8. This tongue-in-cheek vid highlights Zayn's fear of water, and has him wearing some cute inflatable armbands.

Which vid is it? *Kiss You*

HELPING HANDS

THE ONE DIRECTION BOYS KNOW THAT THEY'VE BEEN INCREDIBLY LUCKY TO FIND FAME AND FORTUNE DOING SOMETHING THAT THEY LOVE, SO THEY DON'T FORGET TO GIVE BACK TO THOSE LESS FORTUNATE WHEN THEY CAN. READ THE QUOTES AND STATEMENTS BELOW AND FILL IN WHICH BIG-HEARTED BOY WAS INVOLVED WITH WHICH CHARITY. TURN TO **PAGE 92** TO SEE IF YOU'RE RIGHT.

1. The boys were overwhelmed by the experience of visiting Ghana in Africa for Comic Relief. One of them said: "In everyday life we have little problems that we think are so major and then you go over there and actually see people with real problems ... a general sense of putting things in perspective for me."

Who was it? ...... *Zayn* ......

2. Who celebrated his 19th birthday by teaming up with Boyzone member Keith Duffy for a charity golf tournament to raise money for an autism charity?

Who was it? ...... *Niall* ......

3. This 1D member worked hard to organize a charity soccer game in aid of Bluebell Wood Children's Hospice. His team, the Three Horseshoes, even won!

Who was it? ..... *Louis Tomlinson*

4. "For my birthday I would like everyone to visit *cancerresearchuk.org* and donate as much as they can to help fight cancer." Who tweeted this plea to his fans before his 18th birthday?

Who was it? ..... *Liam.*

5. This band member tweeted how proud he was when his mom climbed Mount Kilimanjaro in Africa for charity, and urged his fans to support her. He also sponsored her £5,000 ($7,683) for her climb, which ended up raising more than £25,000 ($38,415) to support terminally ill children.

Who was it? ..... *Harry*

6. This shy guy was persuaded to go topless, but only if a certain amount of money was raised by a radio station for the Teenage Cancer Trust. Fans could call and donate money, and only if the target was hit would this buff band member release the pic of him with no shirt on.

Who was it? ..... *Zayn.*

7. The 1D boys are a force to be reckoned with when they work as a team. How many of the following did they do to make sure Comic Relief raised as much money as possible?

a. Recorded the official charity single "One Way or Another (Teenage Kicks)" with no payment or royalties

b. Saved money by recording their own video so they could donate more to charity

c. Visited Ghana to publicize the work that Comic Relief does there

d. Appeared on the *Red Nose Day* television show to sing the official single

e. Supported Niall in a sponsored silence

f. Auctioned off the clothes they wore in Ghana

g. Harry made Red Nose cupcakes and shared the recipe so fans could do the same

h. Did something funny for money—including wearing crazy red noses

FACT FILE: NIALL HORAN

HERE ARE FOUR FACTS AND ONE FIB ABOUT NIALL HORAN. PUT A CHECK IN THE BOX BESIDE EACH STATEMENT THAT YOU THINK IS TRUE. PUT AN "X" NEXT TO EACH STATEMENT THAT YOU THINK IS FALSE. THE ANSWERS ARE ON **PAGE 92**.

1. Niall's dad said he always wanted to be a soccer player when he was younger.

2. The singer that Niall would most like to see perform is Michael Bublé.

3. Niall is a supporter of Derby County Football Club.

4. Niall had planned to go to college to learn how to be a sound engineer.

5. Busted was the first big-name band that Niall saw live.

EVERY DIRECTION

THE 1D-ASSOCIATED WORDS BELOW APPEAR IN MORE THAN ONE DIRECTION IN THE WORDSEARCH ON THE OPPOSITE PAGE. THEY COULD GO UP, DOWN, ACROSS, BACKWARD, OR DIAGONALLY. CAN YOU SPOT THEM ALL? THE ANSWERS ARE ON **PAGE 92**.

BLONDIE

"HEART ATTACK"

COMIC RELIEF

BIG TIME RUSH

"KISS YOU"

OLLY MURS

"MOMENTS"

"ONE WAY OR ANOTHER"

CAMRYN

THIS IS US

O	S	E	T	H	H	S	C	E	R	G	N	I	A	W
N	T	A	C	K	E	O	P	G	N	A	L	L	E	R
E	N	O	T	D	A	O	E	S	D	B	A	G	H	W
W	E	G	H	A	R	A	R	F	P	A	M	D	U	S
A	M	B	I	G	T	I	M	E	R	U	S	H	T	R
Y	O	A	S	Q	A	F	K	C	A	E	K	N	L	U
O	M	N	I	U	T	D	A	S	I	D	U	L	P	M
R	A	A	S	S	T	E	L	Y	P	O	R	O	N	Y
A	C	V	U	X	A	A	O	P	Y	E	D	S	T	L
N	T	A	S	T	C	P	O	S	C	M	R	E	W	L
O	H	E	M	G	K	S	S	C	W	A	P	D	E	O
T	B	L	O	N	D	I	E	A	L	L	M	E	F	R
H	P	E	J	X	K	L	B	D	U	P	M	R	A	D
E	F	E	I	L	E	R	C	I	M	O	C	L	Y	G
R	H	F	V	O	O	M	R	S	Q	U	S	C	R	N

AROUND THE WORLD

THE ONE DIRECTION BOYS ARE NOT JUST FABULOUSLY FAMOUS IN THE U.K. SINCE THEY MET ON *THE X FACTOR* BACK IN 2010, THEY HAVE TRAVELED THE WORLD TO MEET THEIR FANS, AND THEIR SONGS HAVE SHOT TO THE TOP OF THE CHARTS ALL ACROSS THE GLOBE. HOW MUCH DO YOU KNOW ABOUT THEIR JET-SETTING JOURNEYS? IF YOU GET STUCK, THE ANSWERS ARE ON **PAGE 92**.

1. Which band member had never traveled outside the U.K. until he joined One Direction and didn't even have a passport?
   a. Liam
   b. Zayn
   c. Louis

2. How did the 1D boys show respect for their Japanese fans as they stepped off the plane in Tokyo?
   a. They bowed to greet the cheering crowd
   b. They wore matching 1D kimonos
   c. They called to their fans in Japanese

3. Two of the boys showed off their surfing skills on their 2012 Australian tour. Which two?

   a. Harry and Liam

   b. Louis and Harry

   (c.) Liam and Louis

4. One Direction are used to flying high in every sense, but what do they say is their favorite way of traveling?

   (a.) Together in the 1D tour bus

   b. Individually by private jet

   c. With friends in a snazzy stretch limo

5. During their first U.S. tour, One Direction had the honor of doing a live TV interview with the famous American talk show host David Letterman. Which other celeb shared the sofa with them during the interview?

   (a.) Dustin Hoffman

   b. Johnny Depp

   c. Taylor Swift

6. One Direction's first visit to Africa was very special, as it was to raise awareness of a charity's work. Which country did the band visit?

   a. Sierra Leone

   b. Botswana

   (c.) Ghana

7. In November 2012, the band traveled in Europe to be presented with a Bambi award for Pop International. Which country presents the Bambis?

    a. Sweden

    (b.) Germany

    c. Italy

8. During their first North American tour, the boys raved about their sell-out gig at MSG. Which famous venue were they talking about?

    (a.) Madison Square Garden

    b. Montana State Gala

    c. Millennium Stage, Georgia

9. Which of the boys admits to doing the most shopping while waiting around at airports?

    a. Liam

    (b.) Louis

    c. Niall

MYSTERY TWEETER

ALL FIVE OF THE BOYS ARE BIG FANS OF THE SOCIAL NETWORKING SITE, TWITTER. CAN YOU GUESS WHICH BAND MEMBER POSTED THE FOLLOWING TWEETS? WRITE YOUR ANSWER AT THE BOTTOM OF THE PAGE THEN CHECK **PAGE 93** TO SEE IF YOU WERE RIGHT.

🐦 Having a great time at the fan convention hope we get to do another soonnnnn :)

....

🐦 Absolute nutter of a taxi driver ATM feels like I'm on a bank job

....

🐦 Wowee #1000DaysOf1D the best 1000 days of my life, spent with the best 4 brothers i could ever of wished for and the best fans ever! #thanku!

....

🐦 Wish I had the confidence to talk to people

....

🐦 I just had monster munch and 2 milky bars
for breakfast

The mystery Tweeter is .... *Liam. Payne* ....

WOULD YOU RATHER ...

WHAT WOULD YOU DO IF YOU HAD THE CHANCE TO SPEND SOME TIME WITH THE BOYS? TAKE A LOOK AT THE OPTIONS BELOW. ALL YOU HAVE TO DO IS PICK YOUR PREFERRED CHOICE FOR EACH SET OF OPTIONS. WHY NOT GET YOUR FRIENDS TO TRY IT, TOO, AND COMPARE YOUR ANSWERS?

Would you rather ...

Be Harry's hairstylist? ⟷ Play guitar with Niall?

Hang out with One Direction backstage? ⟷ Have VIP seats at their show?

Go on a shopping spree with Louis? ⟷ Chill out and watch a movie together?

Go to a fancy restaurant with Liam? ⟷ Have him cook dinner for you and your friends?

Go to a theme park with the boys? ⟷ Hang out at the beach together?

Help the band write a new song? ⟷ Come up with a cool dance routine for them?

Relax on the beach with the band? ⟷ Go paintballing together?

Go surfing with Liam? ⟷ Go skydiving with Harry?

Do a photoshoot with the boys? ⟷ Have an exclusive interview with them?

Have a karaoke party with Harry? ⟷ Go to a formal party with Zayn?

Take a trip to Paris with the boys? ⟷ Go on an adventurous vacation with them?

Paint a portrait of Zayn? ⟷ Have him paint one of you?

Fly in a private jet with Louis? ⟷ Go for a trip on the 1D tour bus?

Go to Liam's birthday party? ⟷ Invite him to come to your birthday party?

Design outfits for the band? ⟷ Design the set for their next concert?

WHO'S YOUR 1D STYLE ICON?

START
It's a seriously bad hair day and there's a party tonight.
Do you ...

... brush it out—who cares about frizz? Big hair is beautiful.

... borrow a hat from your brother and rock the backward baseball cap look.

Which three words best describe your clothing style?

Classic, elegant, timeless.

Bright, bold, trendy.

Which colors make up most of your wardrobe?

All the colors of the rainbow and more.

Neutrals and pastel shades.

SUPER STYLISH!

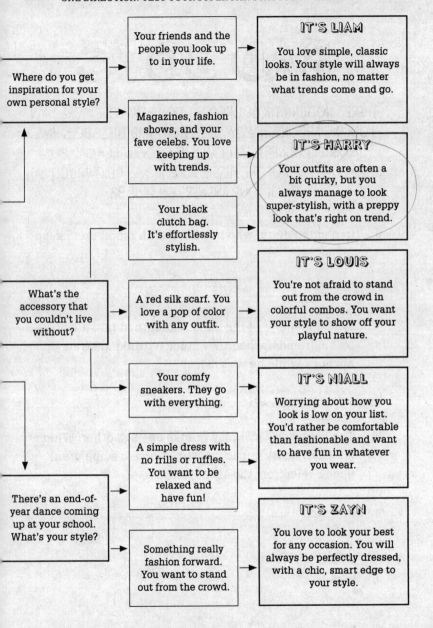

Where do you get inspiration for your own personal style?

Your friends and the people you look up to in your life.

IT'S LIAM

You love simple, classic looks. Your style will always be in fashion, no matter what trends come and go.

Magazines, fashion shows, and your fave celebs. You love keeping up with trends.

IT'S HARRY

Your outfits are often a bit quirky, but you always manage to look super-stylish, with a preppy look that's right on trend.

Your black clutch bag. It's effortlessly stylish.

What's the accessory that you couldn't live without?

A red silk scarf. You love a pop of color with any outfit.

IT'S LOUIS

You're not afraid to stand out from the crowd in colorful combos. You want your style to show off your playful nature.

Your comfy sneakers. They go with everything.

IT'S NIALL

Worrying about how you look is low on your list. You'd rather be comfortable than fashionable and want to have fun in whatever you wear.

A simple dress with no frills or ruffles. You want to be relaxed and have fun!

There's an end-of-year dance coming up at your school. What's your style?

Something really fashion forward. You want to stand out from the crowd.

IT'S ZAYN

You love to look your best for any occasion. You will always be perfectly dressed, with a chic, smart edge to your style.

BAD BOYS

THERE'S NOTHING THOSE ONE DIRECTION BOYS LOVE MORE THAN FOOLING AROUND. NAME A SILLY STUNT AND THESE BOYS HAVE PROBABLY DONE IT! BUT CAN YOU GUESS WHICH BAD BOY COMMITTED EACH OF THE MISCHEVOUS MOVES BELOW? YOU CAN CHECK YOUR ANSWERS ON **PAGE 93**.

1. In a video diary, who had his mouth taped up to keep him quiet?

Answer: _Louis Tomlinson_

2. Which member of the band was turned into a walrus by his friends, when they stuck a drinking straw up his nose while he was asleep?

Answer: _Harry Styles_

3. The boys don't just play pranks on each other. Which famously scary music maestro received some prank phone calls from the 1D boys?

Answer: _Simon Cowell._

4. In which famous area of Los Angeles did the boys jump on two unattended golf carts and go on an unofficial sightseeing tour of the Warner Bros studios?

Answer: *Hollywood*

5. Which member of the band was dared by the others to drink a mixture of mustard, ketchup, coke, and milkshake? Mmm, tasty!

Answer: *Zayn Malik*

6. Who said "Louis regularly breaks into my room and throws buckets of water over me when I'm sleeping."

Answer: *Niall Horan*

7. Which one of the five do they all agree is the laziest?

Answer: *Zayn Malik*

8. At which concert arena did Harry have his pants pulled down by a mischevious Liam while he was belting out a solo on the "Take Me Home" tour?

Answer: *London O2*

GOTTA BE 1D!

FACT FILE: LIAM PAYNE

HERE ARE FOUR FACTS AND ONE FIB ABOUT LIAM PAYNE.
PUT A CHECK IN THE BOX BESIDE EACH STATEMENT THAT YOU
THINK IS TRUE. PUT AN "X" NEXT TO EACH STATEMENT THAT YOU
THINK IS FALSE. THE ANSWERS ARE ON **PAGE 93.**

1. Liam is from Wolverhampton.

2. He once split his pants on stage, revealing his Superman boxer shorts.

3. Liam has a phobia of jelly.

4. Liam's middle name is James.

5. He can play guitar and piano.

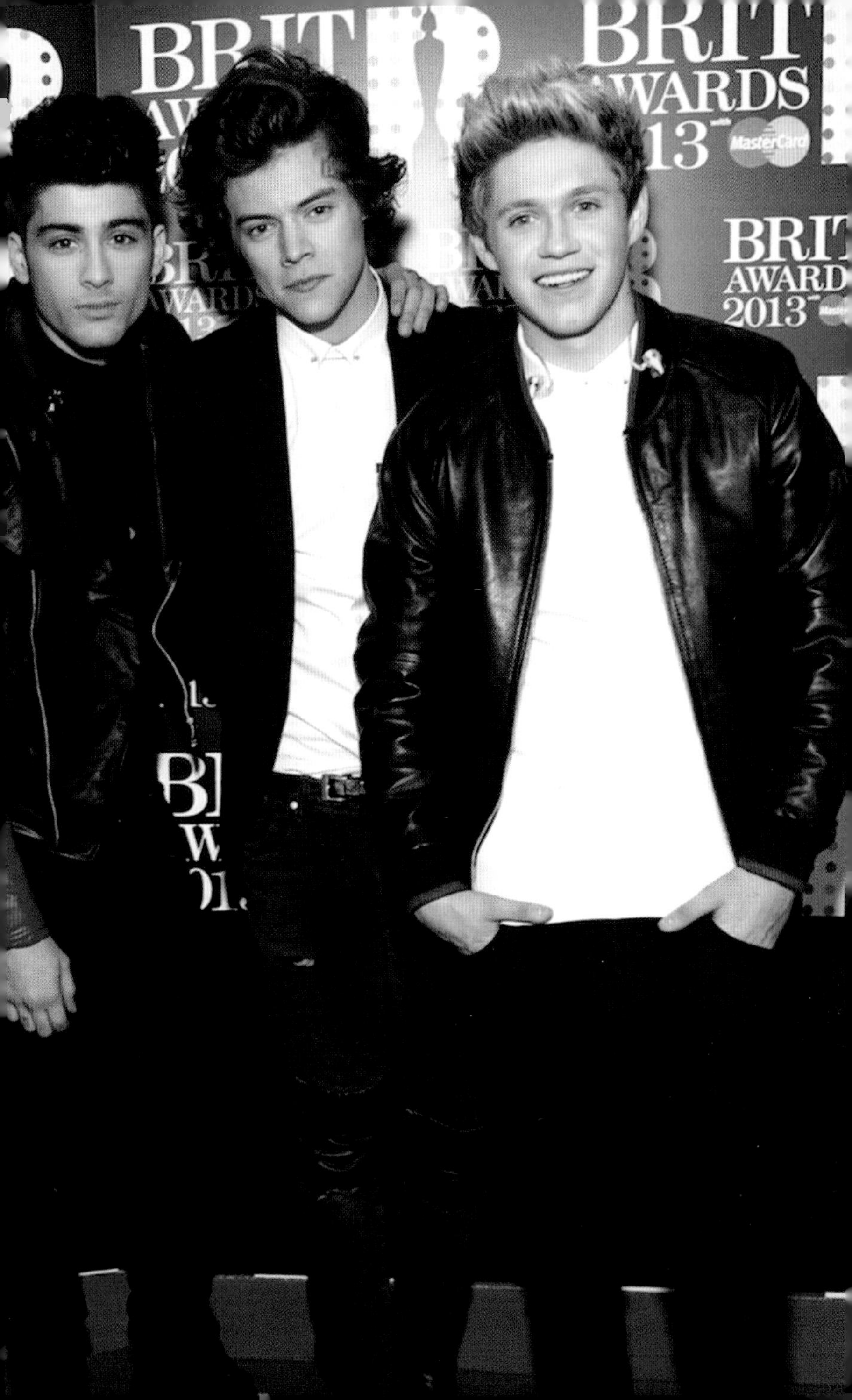
BRIT
AWARDS
2013
MasterCard
BRIT
AWARDS
2013

SPOT THE DIFFERENCE

Can you find eight differences between the top and bottom pictures? You can check your answers on page 93.

MYSTERY TWEETER

CAN YOU GUESS WHICH BAND MEMBER POSTED THE FOLLOWING TWEETS? WRITE YOUR ANSWER AT THE BOTTOM OF THE PAGE THEN CHECK **PAGE 93** TO SEE IF YOUR POWERS OF ONE DIRECTION DETECTION ARE STRONG!

🐦 Hi everyone, just a quick message to say I love all you guys, without your support I don't know what I'd do :) x

....

🐦 Can't get over you guys. Don't get how much you amaze me. Thank you for everything, you truly are the best fans in the world. Love you all x

....

🐦 Buzzing for the show today :D should be good fun x

....

🐦 LA is definitely one of my favorite places to stay love this place :) x

....

🐦 Just before I go to bed just want to say Happy Birthday to one of musics biggest inspirations, Michael Jackson, you truly were a legend RIP x

The mystery Tweeter is .... Zayn. Malik ....

SETLIST SCRAMBLE

IT'S THE FIRST NIGHT OF ONE DIRECTION'S WORLD TOUR, AND THE BOYS ARE ABOUT TO TAKE TO THE STAGE IN FRONT OF THOUSANDS OF THEIR ADORING FANS. BUT THERE'S A PROBLEM... SOMEONE HAS MIXED UP THE SONG TITLES ON THE BOYS' SETLIST, AND NOW THEY CAN'T FIGURE OUT WHAT THEY'RE SUPPOSED TO BE SINGING! CAN YOU UNSCRAMBLE THE SONG TITLES BELOW AND HELP SAVE THE SHOW? ANSWERS ARE ON **PAGE 94**.

1. "ENO GINTH"

One Thing

2. "SALT RIFTS SKIS"

Last First Kiss

3. "EVIL HEWIL REWE GOUNY"

Live While Wer're Young

4. "TOGTA EB UYO"

Gotta Be You

5. "CORK EM"

Rock Me

6. "EARTH CATKAT"

Heart Attack

7. "TILLET NIGHTS"

Little Things

8. "HYTE TOND WONK OTUBA SU"

They Don't Know About Us

9. "EVAS OYU OTTHING"

Save You Tonight

10. "VEOR NAGIA"

Over Again

11. "MURMES VELO"

Summer Love

12. "HECANG YM DIMN"

Change My Mind

SERIOUSLY SPOOKY

IT'S THE MOST EXCITING DAY EVER. YOU ENTERED A COMPETITION TO INTERVIEW ONE DIRECTION—AND WON! FILL IN THE BLANKS IN THE STORY BELOW TO DECIDE WHAT HAPPENS NEXT. YOU CAN USE THE SUGGESTIONS IN BRACKETS TO HELP YOU, OR FILL IN THE BLANKS WITH YOUR OWN CHOICES.

You are being driven in a ...... *station wagon* ......
(sports car/ Rolls Royce /limo) to a mansion where you will interview your favorite band of all time. Bliss!

Soon the drive comes to an end. The car rolls down a sweeping driveway that leads up to a towering stone house. If you're honest, it looks a little creepy. There are ...... *ivy plants growing on the* ......
...... *building* .... (gargoyles over the door/ gravestones in the garden/ plants creeping up the walls)

As soon as you step out of the car, the driver pops his head out of the window. "This place is too spooky for me!" he says before he skids away.

"Wait!" you cry, but it's too late. *Great!* you think, looking up at the ...... *dark windows* .... (thunder clouds/ dark windows/ crumbling roof)

You better get inside. The crew is probably already in there waiting for you.

You knock on the door loudly. No one answers, so you push it gently and it swings open with a groan. You're beginning to wish .... *your mom* .... (your BFF's name) was with you.

As you step into the cold, dusty hallway, you suddenly hear a ..... *big crash* ..... (moaning sound/ big crash/ loud banging) coming from one of the adjoining rooms.

You decide to investigate, so you tiptoe silently into the room where the noise came from.

"Aaaah!" you scream when you enter the room. A giant .... *skeleton* .... (skeleton/ mummy/ zombie) swings down from the doorframe and brushes your shoulders.

"Get off me!" you cry, swatting the horrible thing with your hands. But wait—it's made of rubber. It's just a stupid prop left over from Halloween. Annoyed, but still feeling a little on edge, you decide to search the house. Someone else *must* be here. You head back to the main hallway and up the spiral staircase that creaks and groans under your feet.

"....... *Harry!* ...." (Harry/ Zayn/ Louis/ Liam/ Niall) you shout. "..... *Do you have any snacks?* ....." (Is anyone there?/Hello?/ Come out, please, I'm scared!)

"Help! Help!" you hear a scared voice shriek. Suddenly Harry Styles stumbles out of a bedroom. His white shirt is drenched in a large red stain. You wrinkle your nose—curiously, he smells like ketchup. Harry lurches forward and collapses at your feet. There's no denying it now, you're terrified. You kneel down and lay a hand on his curly hair.

He points feebly down the hall. "I left my phone in the room at the end," he croaks. "Please! Call ....the dentist." (the police/ an ambulance/ my hairdresser)

You promise you will, and Harry lets out a groan of thanks. There isn't a minute to lose. You dart up the hallway and toward the room that Harry was pointing to. As you pass another door, Niall staggers out of it. He's ....licking the floor.
(deathly pale/ unsteady on his feet/ about to start crying)

"Please," he says, clutching at your sweater, "you have to help us." Acting much braver than you feel, you tell Niall that it's going to be okay, and head to the door at the end of the hall. You have to get Harry's phone and save the boys from whatever terrifying thing is happening—if they're all still alive!

It's pitch dark inside the room, and really, really quiet. You can hear ..."Out of the woods" playing down the hall. (your heartbeat / the blood pounding in your ears/ your fast breathing) You have the horrible feeling that you're not alone in here. Something flutters against your arm, making you jump, and there's ..... *a cold breeze* ....

.... (a ghostly wailing sound/ a cold breath on the back of your neck/ floorboards creaking across the room)

Something grabs you by the shoulder and whirls you around. "It's a ghost!" you scream at the top of your lungs. Suddenly, the lights flicker on and in front of you is Louis Tomlinson's smiling face.

"What's going on?" you shriek. "It's okay," says Louis. "It was us all along, pulling a prank on you." Then you notice Liam in the corner of the room, in fits of laughter, pulling a sheet from over his head. "There's your ghost," says Louis with a grin.

Niall and Zayn come into the room, followed by Harry. "It's going to take ages to get this ketchup out of my shirt," he says. "Totally worth it though, *but I didn't get to use my jar of pickles.* ." (you should have seen your face/ I wish we'd had a camera/ best prank yet)

"Seriously though guys, we owe *this raccoon* ..... (your name) an apology," says Zayn. "You were really brave, and we promise we'll give you some real exclusives in the interview. You've earned it!"

SECRET GIG

OMG, YOU'VE FOUND A VIP PASS FOR A TOP-SECRET GIG THAT THE ONE DIRECTION BOYS ARE HOLDING, BUT SOME OF THE VITAL DETAILS ARE MISSING. CAN YOU SOLVE THE CLUES AND FIGURE OUT THE LOCATION OF THE GIG AND WHO THE SPECIAL GUEST WILL BE? YOU CAN CHECK YOUR ANSWERS ON **PAGE 94**.

The gig will be held in the same city that Niall auditioned for *The X Factor*, back in 2010.

Where is it? .... *Dublin* ....

The rumor is that there will be a special guest appearing at the gig. Cross out all the K's, V's, B's and X's to find the answer.

M	K̶	I	L	V̶	E	X̶	B̶	Y
X̶	V̶	C	K̶	Y	B̶	K̶	R	X̶
K̶	X̶	K̶	B̶	V̶	U	B̶	V̶	S

Who is the mystery special guest? ....
.... ~~Hilo~~ *Miley Cyrus*

There's a lock on the door to the backstage area that needs a special combination. Combine the correct answers to these questions and you will have the five-digit code.

1. How many dates are there on One Direction's *Take Me Home* world tour?
   a. 50
   b. 88
   c. 117 *(circled)*

2. Which number is the month of the year of Harry's birthday?
   a. 4
   b. 2 *(circled)*
   c. 11

3. How many bonus tracks are there on the Yearbook edition of *Take Me Home*?
   a. 4 *(circled)*
   b. 10
   c. 7

What's the combination? ......11724......

BIG DREAMS

READ THE STORY BELOW, AND FILL IN THE BLANKS AS YOU GO.
LET ONE DIRECTION'S INCREDIBLE SUCCESS STORY INSPIRE YOU
TO GET OUT THERE AND FOLLOW YOUR DREAMS.

Does this sound familiar? It's late on Saturday afternoon
and you can't stand to be in the house any longer. When
you're not being told to clean your room, someone's
nagging you about doing your homework. Worse, all your
friends are away and the rest of the weekend looks bleak.

You head for your secret corner of the park, settle on
a bench, and shut your eyes to dream about your fave
boy band instead.

"Sorry! We didn't mean to disturb you," says a familiar
voice. You open your eyes and there's ... Louis Tomlinson!

"Wha ... ?" you stammer. "NO!" Behind Louis, four other
familiar faces are grinning at you. And there you are,
wearing your oldest jeans, with your mouth open.

"That's not the reaction we usually get," laughs Harry.

With three boys squeezed onto the bench with you, and
two sitting on the grass, you can hardly breathe. "What are
you doing here?" you gasp.

"Our tour bus is stuck in a traffic jam," Liam explains. "We're just hanging out until it gets here. What are you doing here?"

You explain: *Planning to take over the world, but I haven't acquired enough cats.*

Your woes sound a bit lame when said out loud, but the boys are sympathetic. "It's rough when your friends are away," says Niall. "That's why we're so lucky. When One Direction was put together, we all got instant friends for life."

Well, it's all right for them, you think. They're One Direction!

Zayn seems to have read your mind. "Amazing things will happen for you, too," he says. "What do you dream of?"

You find yourself telling him: *World domination with an army of cats.*

"Wow! That's so cool," says Liam. "You should go for it."

"I don't think it'll ever happen," you say, looking down at the floor.

"Maybe not just like that," says Louis, "but something else might be just round the corner. We didn't get the solo careers we dreamed of. We didn't even win *The X Factor*. But ..."

" ...we're doing all right," says Harry, finishing Louis's sentence with a grin. "There must have been times you were disappointed or stressed but everything turned out okay in the end."

You find yourself telling them about: *All people want to do is drink and party but I want to stay in and enjoy my snacks.*

"And I bet there are some really great things in your life," smiles Niall. "What's good about being you?"

To your surprise, you can suddenly think of loads of things: *I like cats and books and watching good T.V.*

I am particular about who I
choose to spend time with
and I'm funny

You're smiling as you say shyly, "And meeting you guys has been a pretty good thing. Actually, the BEST thing ever."

The boys all give you beaming smiles, and you can feel yourself blushing. At that moment, Harry's phone rings. "The bus is here," he tells the boys. Then he turns to you. "Not so long ago, we were just like you," he says. "Don't stop dreaming."

Suddenly, you find you're alone on a park bench again. Did that really just happen? You wish you'd had your camera with you so you could have snapped a pic and showed your friends. You're feeling so much better, and really grateful to the guys for cheering you up. Before you head for home, you make a few resolutions. Write them here. Your dreams are on their way!

Read more
Take care of yourself.
Drink water
LOVE! ♡
Spend less time on social
media ";

THE BLUSH FACTOR

EACH ONE OF THESE EMBARRASSING FACTS AND CRINGE-WORTHY TALES IS BOUND TO MAKE A BAND MEMBER BLUSH. CAN YOU GUESS WHICH ONE? WRITE A NAME BELOW EACH FACT, THEN TURN TO **PAGE 94** FOR THE ANSWERS.

1. He ran to help a New Zealand fan who appeared to be having trouble breathing, only to find that the band was being pranked by U.K. TV hosts Ant and Dec on their Saturday night show.

Who was it? ...... *Harry Styles*

2. On the final night of his school play *Grease*, this band member was dared by friends to moon the audience. The next day his mom got a note that said, "Your son has been excluded for three days for baring his bottom."

Who was it? ...... *Louis Tomlinson.*

3. He admits to talking in his sleep "all the time."

Who was it? ...... *Niall Horan*

4. His first kiss was with a girl much taller than him so he stood on a brick before puckering up.

Who was it? _Zayn Malik_

5. This boy once confessed: "My hair straighteners are pink! I have to use them or my hair would be out of control."

Who was it? _Liam Payne_

6. One of the boys has this cringe-tastic story to tell: "Once I was in the bath and Louis told me he needed something so, being stupidly gullible, I opened the door and he was waiting with an ITV2 camera crew outside. I was starkers."

Who was it? _Niall Horan_

7. He used to have a recurring dream in which he would forget to put clothes on and go to school naked.

Who was it? _Louis Tomlinson_

8. When asked to name what he found most embarrassing, this guy said: "Anything that involves dancing. Anything dance related is awful for me."

Who was it? _Zayn Malik_

9. After a party at JLS, star Marvin Humes's house in London, this guy was so sleepy that he curled up and went to sleep in a dog bed.

Who was it? ..... *Harry Styles.* .....

10. While performing to a sell-out arena in the U.K., this boy managed to drop his microphone. Oops! What was even worse was that it rolled under the stage and he couldn't get it back.

Who was it? ..... *Liam Payne* .....

11. It must be scary performing in front of so many people every night while on tour, and it's no wonder that nerves sometimes get the better of the boys. Which 1D boy completely forgot the words to his solo during their cover of "Teenage Dirtbag" while on stage? He admitted his mistake and apologized to the crowd, before joining in again with the chorus. Aww!

Who was it? ..... *Louis Tomlinson* .....

FOREVER YOUNG

FACT FILE: LOUIS TOMLINSON

HERE ARE FOUR FACTS AND ONE FIB ABOUT LOUIS TOMLINSON. PUT A CHECK IN THE BOX BESIDE EACH STATEMENT THAT YOU THINK IS TRUE. PUT AN "X" NEXT TO EACH STATEMENT THAT YOU THINK IS FALSE. THE ANSWERS ARE ON **PAGE 94**.

1. The first word Louis spoke as a baby was "cat."

2. Louis has twin sisters named Phoebe and Daisy.

3. He can play the piano.

4. When Louis was six, the Queen visited his primary school in Doncaster and he gave her some flowers.

5. He says he likes girls who eat carrots.

QUIZ TIME

TAKE THIS TEST TO SEE HOW HOT YOUR ONE DIRECTION KNOWLEDGE IS. CHECK YOUR ANSWERS ON **PAGE 94** THEN USE THE SCORECARD ON **PAGE 68** TO RATE YOUR DIRECTIONER DEDICATION.

1. What was the name of the band Louis was in when he was at school?

a. The Rogue
b. The Ready Steady Gos
c. Rumpelstiltskin

2. Which three band members wrote "Last First Kiss?"

a. Liam, Niall, and Zayn
b. Harry, Liam, and Zayn
c. Liam, Zayn, and Louis

3. Which childhood film is one of Harry's all time faves?

a. Mary Poppins
b. The Lion King
c. The Jungle Book

4. What does Liam have a phobia of?

a. Cheese
b. Spoons
c. Monkeys

5. One Direction made a guest appearance on a Nickelodeon TV show. What was it?

   a. Victorious
   b. Allen Surf Girls
   c. iCarly

6. Niall's dad, Bobby, is really proud of his superstar son. What does Bobby do for a living?

   a. Butcher
   b. Lawyer
   c. Taxi driver

7. In which subject did clever Zayn take his exams a whole year early?

   a. Math
   b. History
   c. English

8. Which member of 1D can be seen wearing an orange sweater in the video for "Gotta Be You?"

   a. Liam
   b. Niall
   c. Harry

9. Whose catchphrase is "Vas happenin?"

   a. Louis
   b. Zayn
   c. Harry

10. Which member of 1D is a massive fan of the shoe brand Toms?

    a. Louis

    b. Liam

    c. Zayn

11. How many of the boys have the astrological sign Capricorn?

    a. One

    b. Two

    c. Three

SUPER-FAN SCORECARD

SCORE 0-4
You're just starting out on your 1D journey, and there's so much more to learn. Luckily for you, this kind of homework is never a chore.

SCORE 5-8
There's some definite super-fan potential here, keep up with your 1D studies and you'll be hitting the heights in no time.

SCORE 9-11
Go straight to the top of the class! You really are a super-fan. Reward yourself for your dedication by watching more 1D videos.

MYSTERY TWEETER

READ THESE TWEETS, AND SEE IF YOU CAN FIGURE OUT WHO POSTED THEM. WRITE YOUR ANSWER AT THE BOTTOM OF THE PAGE THEN CHECK **PAGE 95** TO SEE IF YOU WERE RIGHT.

🐦 Time off done! we're heading for the rest of Europe! First stop Paris! Lets do this! Love this country beautiful place! Beautiful fans!

🐦 Got me bus slippers on! the driver got them for us as a present!

🐦 Aaaaagggghhhh! Just woke up to find out I have 11million followers! Thank you soo much to every one of you! Love u all

🐦 Seen a sign in the audience last night! That said "thank you for everything" and I was thinkin NO! THANK YOU FOR EVERYTHING!

🐦 best day off ever....did absolutely nothing! sat on the couch all day! then just drove to mcdonalds and stuffed my face

The mystery Tweeter is .... Niall Horan ....

WHO'S YOUR 1D BFF?

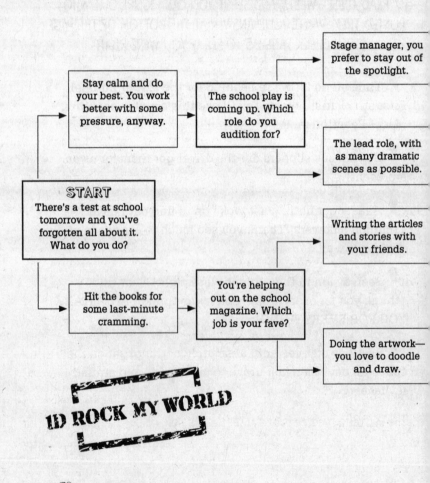

Stay calm and do your best. You work better with some pressure, anyway.

The school play is coming up. Which role do you audition for?

Stage manager, you prefer to stay out of the spotlight.

The lead role, with as many dramatic scenes as possible.

START
There's a test at school tomorrow and you've forgotten all about it. What do you do?

Writing the articles and stories with your friends.

Hit the books for some last-minute cramming.

You're helping out on the school magazine. Which job is your fave?

Doing the artwork—you love to doodle and draw.

1D ROCK MY WORLD

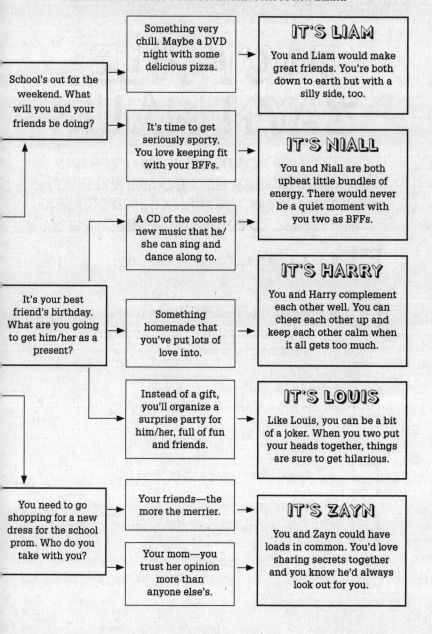

School's out for the weekend. What will you and your friends be doing?

Something very chill. Maybe a DVD night with some delicious pizza.

IT'S LIAM

You and Liam would make great friends. You're both down to earth but with a silly side, too.

It's time to get seriously sporty. You love keeping fit with your BFFs.

IT'S NIALL

You and Niall are both upbeat little bundles of energy. There would never be a quiet moment with you two as BFFs.

A CD of the coolest new music that he/she can sing and dance along to.

IT'S HARRY

You and Harry complement each other well. You can cheer each other up and keep each other calm when it all gets too much.

It's your best friend's birthday. What are you going to get him/her as a present?

Something homemade that you've put lots of love into.

Instead of a gift, you'll organize a surprise party for him/her, full of fun and friends.

IT'S LOUIS

Like Louis, you can be a bit of a joker. When you two put your heads together, things are sure to get hilarious.

You need to go shopping for a new dress for the school prom. Who do you take with you?

Your friends—the more the merrier.

IT'S ZAYN

You and Zayn could have loads in common. You'd love sharing secrets together and you know he'd always look out for you.

Your mom—you trust her opinion more than anyone else's.

FACT FILE: ZAYN MALIK

HERE ARE FOUR FACTS AND ONE FIB ABOUT ZAYN MALIK.
PUT A CHECK IN THE BOX BESIDE EACH STATEMENT THAT YOU
THINK IS TRUE. PUT AN "X" NEXT TO EACH STATEMENT THAT YOU
THINK IS FALSE. YOU CAN FIND THE ANSWERS ON **PAGE 95**.

1. Zayn is from Guildford in Surrey.

2. Before One Direction, Zayn planned to go to college to study English and become a teacher.

3. If Zayn could be an animal, he would like to be a monkey.

4. Zayn's fave boy band is *NSYNC.

5. Zayn's name means "beautiful."

THE FAME GAME

TAKE THIS QUIZ AND GET READY TO DISCOVER YOUR INNER SUPERSTAR. WILL YOU BE A SMASH-HIT SINGER, A STAGE STARLET, OR A TV DIVA? FIND OUT ON **PAGES 76-77.**

1. It's your best friend's birthday party and you're running really late. What do you do?

   a. Stop off on the way to buy her a bunch of flowers as an apology—it might make you even later, but you know she'll appreciate it.

   b. Don't sweat it, loads of her other friends will be there already. Besides, it's fashionable to be late.

   c. Make sure your entrance is as dramatic as possible—people will be so impressed they won't even notice how late you are.

2. What's your fave subject at school?

   a. Music

   b. Whichever lesson lets you sit with your friends

   c. Drama

3. Your folks are letting you choose where to go on your family vacation this year. Where do you pick?

 a. Somewhere with tons of fun activities going on. You want to try your hand at diving and tennis, oh, and cooking, and maybe bungee jumping.

 b. It's got to have a pool, you haven't bought two new super-stylish bikinis for nothing.

 c. Somewhere quiet and relaxing, where you can all spend some quality time together.

4. What is your favorite hobby?

 a. Singing. In the rain, in the shower, in the classroom, anywhere you go, there's always a song going around and around in your head.

 b. Shopping. That counts as a hobby, right?

 c. You just love to keep moving. Whether it's playing sports or dancing the night away, you're always a bundle of energy.

5. Fame is just around the corner—you feel sure of it. How are you going to be discovered as the Next Big Thing?

 a. YouTube. The vids you've uploaded of you singing are just waiting to be spotted by someone in the business.

 b. Every minute is an opportunity to be discovered—that's why it's so important that you look your best at all times.

 c. You've just landed the lead in the school play, and you're practicing like crazy to impress any talent scouts in the audience.

6. If you could be any animal, what would you be?
   a. A feisty and fabulous lion
   b. A pampered pooch
   c. A curious and intelligent bird

7. Where would you like to live?
   a. In a big, buzzing city with loads to keep you busy
   b. You don't care where it is, but your house has to be amazing—full of gadgets and with enough room for some serious parties
   c. At home, near your family and old friends

8. How would your friends describe you?
   a. Caring and thoughtful
   b. Bubbly and funny
   c. Confident and creative

9. You're going to see your fave band in concert. How will you get noticed?
   a. You'll arrive super early and hang out by the tour bus, singing their songs and hoping they hear you.
   b. You've planned a fabulous outfit and you're ready to fight your way to the front row.
   c. You and your friends have spent ages making banners and posters—they're so bright and sparkly that the band are sure to spot them from the stage.

Turn the page to discover your inner superstar ...

THE RESULTS

Count up the number of a's, b's, and c's you marked in the quiz on **pages 73 to 75**. Then find out your inner superstar, and which celeb is your star role model, below.

MOSTLY A'S: SMASH-HIT SINGER

Music is your passion, and if you're ever feeling blue, you know that listening to your fave song will soon put a smile back on your face. You're creative and driven, and you always have a notebook with you so you can scribble down new thoughts and lyrics. You know that fame and fortune require lots of hard work, and you've researched the stars you admire so you can figure out how to recreate their success.

YOUR STAR ROLE MODEL IS: JUSTIN BIEBER

Justin is the undisputed prince of pop, and his fans adore him. He works really hard, and for him it's all about the music. You've got that same passion and dedication, so keep dreaming and keep singing, and one day you'll get to the top.

1D ARE THE BEST!

MOSTLY B'S: TV DIVA

Your sparkling personality means you're the perfect candidate for a starring role on screen. You're loud and proud, and your friends all know that there's sure to be excitement and more than just a little bit of drama with you around. You'll put the work into the things you're passionate about, but most of all you want to have fun.

YOUR STAR ROLE MODEL IS: KATY PERRY

You love Katy's quirky sense of style, and the fact that she dares to be different. Like you, she's super outgoing and bubbly, and she loves to be the center of attention. You can't wait until the day you've got photographers asking if you're ready for your close-up.

MOSTLY C'S: STAGE STARLET

Normally you're quite shy and happy to be in the background, but when you get out on that stage, everyone can see you blossom. You love to act and spend hours people watching to bring your characters to life.

YOUR STAR ROLE MODEL IS: EMMA WATSON

You really admire the Harry Potter star's grace and poise, and her attitude toward fame. When you hit the heights of superstardom, your down-to-earth and intelligent outlook will help you to handle your celebrity status just as well as Emma.

BOWLING BOYS

READ THE FUN STORY BELOW AND FILL IN THE BLANKS TO CREATE YOUR OWN ONE DIRECTION ADVENTURE. YOU CAN USE THE WORDS IN BRACKETS, OR FILL IN THE BLANKS WITH YOUR OWN CHOICES.

Some of your friends make fun of you for your rather different hobby, but you don't care. To you, bowling is the best sport in the world, and you're pretty good at it, too! So good in fact, that today you are competing in the final for the regional championship with your team, The ....

.... (Hot Shots/ Pinheads/ Rolling Pins)
You just have to win!

While you wait for the host to announce the opposing

team, you're busy ....

....

.... (buffing your glittery bowling ball/ polishing your hot-pink bowling shoes/ straightening your team T-shirt)

Suddenly the host pipes up. "Ladies and gentlemen!" he says. "We have a little surprise for you today. I am pleased to introduce a special celebrity team that will be playing today. Please welcome to the lanes ... One Direction!"

Your ....
(jaw drops to the floor/ legs turn to jelly/ stomach feels full of butterflies) You can't believe you have to bowl against One Direction. You look around at your teammates. They too look shocked beyond belief.

"It's okay, guys," you say "..
...." (We can do this/ I've heard they are terrible bowlers/ Surely they can't bowl as well as they sing)

The crowd goes wild as Harry, Niall, Liam, Zayn, and Louis enter the room. They look .... (gorgeous/ cute/ funny) in their matching red and blue striped T-shirts.

.... (Harry/ Niall/ Liam/ Zayn/ Louis) winks at you as he takes his place on the bench opposite of yours.

....
("Good luck!" "May the best team win,"/ "You look cute in a bowling outfit") he says, with a smile.

"Let the bowling begin!" the host cries.

You gulp loudly. You're up first, but your ....
....
(knees are trembling/ hands are shaking/ brain feels fuzzy)

Your first throw goes straight down the gutter and you almost stamp your foot in frustration. You haven't thrown a gutter ball in years. It's all One Direction's fault.

On your second turn, you aim your ball straight down the middle. It glides down the lane but only manages to knock over .... (two/ three/ five) pins. You must do better next time.

When you take your seat again, ...
(Harry/ Niall/ Liam/ Zayn/ Louis) gets up to bowl. He turns to you as he picks up his ball.

"Better luck next time!" he grins.

Okay, so his smile is pretty amazing, but you're so mad you could scream. You fold your arms and turn your head away.

Luckily, your teammates don't seem to be as affected as you at bowling against the 1D boys—obviously they aren't super-fans like you are. Your scores are soon tied.

Soon it's your turn again and only a strike will be good enough. You have to push your team into the lead. You watch as Harry maneuvers a clever curving ball that gives him a spare. He ....
(punches the air/ gives Louis a high five/ whoops excitedly) and sits down.

You take your place at the lane and feel confident as you swing your ball. But—oh no!—it only knocks down half of the pins. On your next turn you manage to get the rest of the pins down, but you were sure you'd get a strike that time.

Next up is .... (Niall/ Liam/ Zayn/ Louis) He
rolls the ball into the pins, knocking them all down. He
gives you a cocky ....
(wink/ smile/ thumbs up) "That's how it's done," he teases.

"How about a little bet?" you ask him. "If we win, you
have to perform a private concert for me and my team, but
if you win, we have to ....
...." (polish your bowling balls/ clean
your shoes/ donate money to your favorite charity)

"Deal," he says and takes a seat with the rest of the band.

Excitedly, you tell your teammates that if you can win this
game then you'll get your very own One Direction concert.

"That's amazing!" they all chorus together. "We have to
win."

Soon, it's the last turn of the game. The scores are even
and it's all down to you. You try to zone out the cheering
crowd and think of something that makes you happy. But
what makes you happy? Of course, your favorite 1D song!

You close your eyes and sing ....
.... (your favorite 1D song) in your head, and you feel
instantly calmer. You roll your ball and—YES!—a strike.
You've won the game!

As your team runs to hug you, you turn to ....
(Harry/ Niall/ Liam/ Zayn/ Louis) and say, "*That's* how
it's done!"

FAN FRENZY

ONE DIRECTION ARE LUCKY ENOUGH TO HAVE MILLIONS OF FANS AND FOLLOWERS ALL ACROSS THE GLOBE, AND THEY'RE SO THANKFUL TO EACH AND EVERY ONE OF THEIR DEDICATED DIRECTIONERS–THAT INCLUDES YOU, OF COURSE! SOMETIMES THOUGH, THINGS CAN GET A LITTLE BIT CRAZY. SEE IF YOU CAN COMPLETE THE FRENZIED FAN FACTS BELOW, AND CHECK YOUR ANSWERS ON **PAGE 95**.

1. One fan was so determined to get past security and meet the band that she hid for hours in a very unusual place. Where was it?
   a. A public toilet
   b. A garbage can
   c. A bush

2. The boys get sent lots of gifts from their fans, and most of them are super cute. Sometimes though, they're just bizarre. Harry said that the weirdest gift he received was a box of what?
   a. Mushrooms carved to look like the band
   b. 42 eyelashes
   c. A half-eaten piece of toast with chocolate spread on it

3. When the boys arrived at a station in Paris, they were mobbed by a huge crowd of screaming fans. Liam lost a part of his outfit in the crush. What was it?

a. His hat

b. His shoe

c. His sunglasses

4. The 1D boys would all love to have a pet to take on the road with them, but which bizarre live animal was Louis once sent as a gift?

a. A gecko

b. A giant snail

c. A hermit crab

5. It's normal when meeting new people to shake their hand, give them a hug, or maybe even a kiss on the cheek. What over-the-top greeting did a fan try out on Liam once?

a. They licked his face

b. They tried to give him a piggy back

c. They ruffled his hair

NAME THAT TUNE

IT'S TIME TO TEST YOUR 1D TUNE TRIVIA AND SOLVE THESE CROSSWORD CLUES. IF YOU GET STUCK, THE ANSWERS ARE ON **PAGE 95**.

ACROSS

2. This track on *Take Me Home* was co-written by all five of the 1D boys (6, 4)

4. This upbeat track from the boys' first album mentions pop diva Katy Perry (2, 3, 5)

6. In this fantastic track, it's blonde cutie Niall who takes the lead vocals in the chorus (4, 2)

DOWN

1. The hilarious video for this hit song shows the boys skiing and surfing (4, 3)

3. This song is seriously catchy. It was the B-side to 'What Makes You Beautiful," can you name it? (2, 2, 2)

5. Brit band McFly stepped in to help write this track on *Take Me Home* (1, 5)

7. This track appears as a bonus in the deluxe edition of *Take Me Home* released for U.S. store, Target (5)

1. Kissyou
2. S
4. UPAllNIght

CENTER STAGE

GRAB A COUPLE OF FRIENDS AND SOME DICE, AND GET READY TO PLAY THIS ONE DIRECTION GAME. IT'S SURE TO HAVE YOU ALL IN FITS OF LAUGHTER. HERE'S HOW TO PLAY.

1. Each player should pick two numbers between one and six, and should write their names in the spaces next to their chosen numbers on chart A on **page 87**.

2. Decide who will go first. The chosen player rolls the dice. The number she rolls represents the player who must face the challenge.

3. She should then roll the dice again. Match the number she rolls to the song listed in chart B.

4. She rolls again, and matches that number to chart C, then again, for chart D.

5. The player that was chosen with the first roll will now have to perform the song from chart B, in the style from chart C, and with the extras from chart D. For example, if a 1, then a 3, then a 6 was rolled, she would have to sing "One Thing" in a French accent, while brushing her teeth!

A. PLAYERS' NAMES

1. ....
2. ....
3. ....
4. ....
5. ....
6. ....

B. SONG TITLES

1. "One Thing"
2. "Kiss You"
3. "Little Things"
4. "Up All Night"
5. "Tell Me A Lie"
6. "I Would"

C. SINGING STYLES

1. Whispering
2. Shouting
3. In a French accent
4. Backward
5. In a really deep voice
6. Sped up

D. EXTRAS

1. Jogging round the room
2. With clenched teeth
3. Wearing a hat
4. Jumping up and down
5. Making funny faces
6. Brushing your teeth

MYSTERY TWEETER

USE YOUR SLEUTHING SKILLS TO WORK OUT WHICH BAND MEMBER POSTED THE FOLLOWING TWEETS. WRITE YOUR ANSWER AT THE BOTTOM OF THE PAGE THEN CHECK **PAGE 95** TO SEE HOW YOU DID.

🐦 I slept on my shoulder, now my left arm is numb and is just hanging. It seems to be about 4 inches longer than my right. Cool.

....

🐦 The difference between doing something and not doing something is doing something.

....

🐦 Just had my first ice bath. Note: If someone is laughing as you're getting into something, you probably should stop getting in.

....

🐦 The amount of time you guys put in to doing things for us is amazing. So again, thank you for everything you've done. It feels nice, love. x

The mystery Tweeter is ....*Harry Styles*..........

ALL THE ANSWERS

Super-Fan-Tastic
Pages 6–8

1. c
2. c
3. a
4. b
5. c
6. a
7. b
8. c
9. a
10. b
11. b
12. c

Fact File: Harry Styles
Page 9
The fib is fact number four

Direction Detection
Pages 10–11

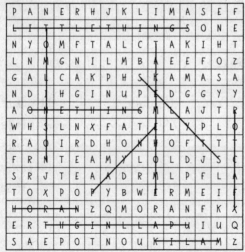

Who Said It?
Pages 12–14

1.	Niall	6.	Zayn	11.	Harry
2.	Liam	7.	Liam	12.	Louis
3.	Harry	8.	Liam	13.	Louis
4.	Niall	9.	Zayn	14.	Niall
5.	Louis	10.	Liam		

Number Knowledge
Page 15

1.	13	3.	3	5.	15
2.	1	4.	21	6.	2

Tattoo Trivia
Pages 16–17

1.	Zayn	3.	Louis	5.	Harry	7.	Louis
2.	Harry	4.	Zayn	6.	Liam	8.	Liam

Spot The Fakes
Pages 18–19

1.	True	6.	False	11.	True
2.	False	7.	False	12.	False
3.	False	8.	False	13.	True
4.	False	9.	True	14.	False
5.	True	10.	False	15.	False

Crack That Crossword
Pages 24–25

Mystery Tweeter
Page 26
The mystery Tweeter is Louis

How Romantic
Pages 28–29

1. Harry   3. Liam   5. Louis   7. Zayn
2. Zayn   4. Niall   6. Harry   8. Louis

Video Stars
Pages 30–31

1. "One Thing"   5. "Gotta Be You"
2. "What Makes You Beautiful"   6. "Kiss You"
3. "One Way Or Another"   7. "Little Things"
4. "Live While We're Young"   8. "Kiss You"

Helping Hands
Pages 32–34

1. Zayn
2. Niall
3. Louis
4. Liam

5. Harry
6. Zayn
7. Yep, you've guessed it, those generous 1D boys did all of these things for Comic Relief!

Fact File: Niall Horan
Page 35
The fib is fact number one

Every Direction
Pages 36–37

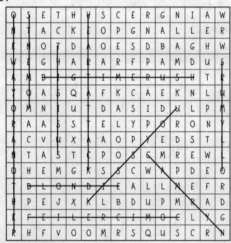

Around The World
Page 38–40

1. b
2. b
3. c
4. a
5. a
6. c
7. b
8. a
9. b

Mystery Tweeter
Page 41
The mystery Tweeter is Liam

Bad Boys
Pages 46–47

1.	Louis	5.	Zayn
2.	Harry	6.	Niall
3.	Simon Cowell	7.	Zayn
4.	Hollywood	8.	London O2

Fact File: Liam Payne
Page 48
The fib is fact number three

Spot The Difference
In Picture Section
1. The stars on the drum are green
2. The rubber duck is missing a blue spot
3. The number on Louis's glasses has changed
4. Zayn's hand is missing
5. Harry is missing a label on his shirt
6. Liam has no stick to hit the xylophone
7. Zayn has lost his gold microphone
8. Niall's sleeve has been turned black

Mystery Tweeter
Page 49
The mystery Tweeter is Zayn

Setlist Scramble
Pages 50–51

1. "One Thing"
2. "Last First Kiss"
3. "Live While We're Young"
4. "Gotta Be You"
5. "Rock Me"
6. "Heart Attack"
7. "Little Things"
8. "They Don't Know About Us"
9. "Save You Tonight"
10. "Over Again"
11. "Summer Love"
12. "Change My Mind"

Secret Gig
Pages 56–57
The gig is taking place in: Dublin
The special guest is: Miley Cyrus
The secret combination is: 11724

The Blush Factor
Pages 62–64

1. Harry
2. Louis
3. Niall
4. Zayn
5. Liam
6. Niall
7. Louis
8. Zayn
9. Harry
10. Liam
11. Louis

Fact File: Louis Tomlinson
Page 65
The fib is fact number four

Quiz Time
Pages 66–68

1. a
2. c
3. b
4. b
5. c
6. a
7. c
8. c
9. b
10. a
11. b

Mystery Tweeter
Page 69
The mystery Tweeter is Niall

Fact File: Zayn Malik
Page 72
The fib is fact number one

Fan Frenzy
Pages 82–83

1. b   3. b   5. a
2. a   4. c

Name That Tune
Pages 84–85

Mystery Tweeter
Page 88
The mystery Tweeter is Harry

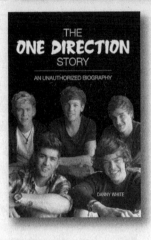